Introduction

Animal stories never fail to delight children. From nursery classics like *The Three Bears* and *The Three Little Pigs*, through Beatrix Potter's timeless *Tale of Peter Rabbit*, right up to such contemporary favourites as Eric Hill's *Spot* books, animal stories have had a unique ability to capture children's imaginations. Part of the reason may be that animal characters, especially those that talk, act and wear clothes like people, transcend human differences of race, colour and class, and provide children with a nonthreatening reflection of their own lives. Children can identify with animal characters in ways they cannot with humans.

Of course, another reason children are drawn to animal stories is that most storybook animals are cute, lovable, appealing and often funny – just like children themselves! And never have animal characters been more cute, lovable and appealing than they are in this collection, enchantingly illustrated by Peter Stevenson. Animal Stories brings together twenty-seven original, entertaining tales and rhymes about all sorts of irresistible, child-friendly animals: rabbits, kittens, puppies, penguins, ducks – there's even a tree-climbing crocodile and a resourceful young dragon! Each story and rhyme is perfect for reading aloud and sharing, at bedtime or anytime, and each is guaranteed to bring delighted demands for more!

Acknowledgments

Stories and rhymes in this book were previously published by Ladybird Books Ltd as follows: The Duck Who Didn't Like Rain in *Storytime for 3 Year Olds*; Mervyn's Glasses, An Up and Down Story in *Storytime for 5 Year Olds*; The Dirty Dinosaur in *Storytime for 2 Year Olds*; The Rainbow Rabbits, Slippy and the Skaters, The Trouble With Babies, Mrs Bunny Had Twins, The Dancing Bunny, Everard's Ears in *Two Minute Bunny Tales*; The Kitten and the Kangaroo, The Roly Poly Kitten in *Two Minute Kitten Tales*; Chickens, The Chewalong Song in *Farmyard Stories for Under Fives*; Brown Bear's Visit, The Runaway Mouse in *Bedtime Stories for Under Fives*; The Puppy Who Went Exploring, The Puppy Who Wanted to Be a Cat in *Two Minute Puppy Tales*; Teamwork, Flop Learns to Swim, Crocodiles *Do Climb Trees* in *Animal Stories for Under Fives*; Dance of the Dolphins in *Storytime for 6 Year Olds*; Just the Job for a Dragon in *Storytime for 4 Year Olds*.

Stories in this book previously published by Ladybird Books Inc, Auburn, Maine, as follows: A Balloon for Katie Kitten, Scaredy Kitten in *Kitten Tales*, Cry Bunny and Scaredy Cat (original title, *Cry Bunny*), New Boots for Rabbit in *Bunny Tales*.

Ladybird books are widely available, but in case of difficulty may be ordered by post or telephone from:
Ladybird Books – Cash Sales Department Littlegate Road Paignton Devon TQ3 3BE Telephone 01803 554761

A catalogue record for this book is available from the British Library

Published by Ladybird Books Ltd Loughborough Leicestershire UK
Ladybird Books Inc Auburn Maine 04210 USA

ANIMAL STORIES

Chosen by Ronne Randall
Illustrated by Peter Stevenson

Contents

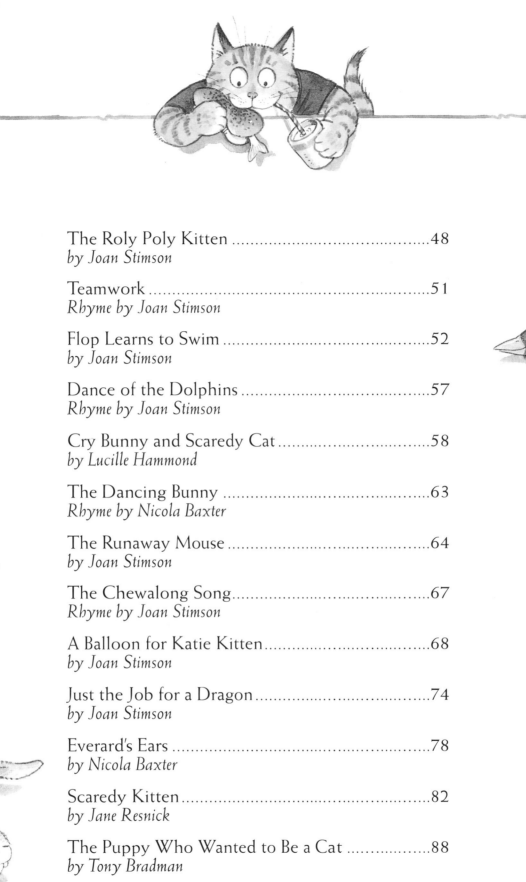

New Boots for Rabbit

One morning Rabbit looked outside and saw that it was raining. He remembered his new boots, and he hurried to put them on.

"It's raining out," said Rabbit to his mother. "Let's go for a walk so I can wear my new boots."

But Rabbit's mother was busy, and she said, "In a little while, Rabbit, when I finish my work."

So Rabbit began to play on his own, with his new boots on.

"With these boots," he whispered, "I could walk into a river and catch the biggest fish in the whole world." And he pretended he was a fisherman pulling in a huge fish.

Then Rabbit said to his mother, "Is it time to go for a walk now?"

"Later," replied his mother, because she was still busy.

So Rabbit played on his own some more.

"With these boots," he said, "I could be a sailor in a storm, travelling all over the world." And he pretended he was in a boat, tossing on the sea.

When he had finished playing, he called to his mother, "Are you ready yet?"

"Not quite," answered his mother.

One more time Rabbit went off to play.

"With these boots," he said, "I could be an explorer in the jungle." And he imagined himself walking through a rain forest, discovering birds and animals.

At last Rabbit heard his mother say, "Time to go now!" So, together, they went out for a walk.

But what a surprise! The rain had stopped, and the sun was drying up the puddles. Rabbit was so disappointed and cross that he felt like crying. He had waited all that time to get his new boots wet, and now the sun was shining!

Rabbit and his mother kept walking until they reached the park. Rabbit began to feel a bit better. He and his mother could look at the fountain with the little pool all around it, and that was always fun.

Suddenly someone shouted, "Oh, dear me, help!"

It was an elegant lady in smart clothes, and her hat had blown into the fountain.

"I'll get it!" said Rabbit, and quickly he waded into the little pool to rescue the hat.

"Oh, thank you," said the elegant lady when Rabbit returned the hat. "How lucky that you were wearing your boots." She smiled at Rabbit. "With boots like those, maybe someday you'll be a fisherman, or a sailor, or even an explorer!"

On the way home Rabbit felt very pleased and proud, and he skipped along in his new, wet boots. "With boots like these," he thought, "who knows *what* might happen?"

The Duck Who Didn't Like Rain

Derek was a new duckling. He lived with his family by the Big Pond.

Mr and Mrs Duck were proud of their ducklings. Every morning they took them for a long walk.

It was a long, dry spring that year. But at last it rained. And that's when the trouble started.

Mrs Duck was excited to see the rain. She lifted her wing carefully and woke the ducklings. "Look, children," she said. "It's a lovely wet day!"

The ducklings rubbed the sleep from their eyes. "Is that the rain you told us about, Mum?" they asked, beeping with excitement.

"Yes, indeed," she said. "Now hurry and line up. Your father's ready to go!"

"Let us proceed!" cried Mr Duck, and the Duck family set off in a long line. But Derek lagged behind.

"What is it, dear?" asked his mother gently.

"Don't like it," said Derek in a small voice. "Don't like the rain. Makes my toes feel tickly."

"Makes your *toes* feel tickly?" cried Derek's father. "Whoever heard of a duckling with tickly toes?"

Mrs Duck didn't shout. That evening she paid a visit to Old Ma Goat. Ma Goat kept a shop, and she sold almost everything you could think of.

Mrs Duck was in luck. Ma Goat had some wellingtons, just the right size for Derek.

Next time it rained, Mrs Duck gave Derek the wellingtons.

"Let us depart!" cried Mr Duck.

"How's that, Derek?" asked Mrs Duck gently.

"Still don't like it," whispered Derek. "Musses up my feathers. Spoils my hair."

"Spoils your *hair*?" cried Derek's father. He was very upset to have a child who worried about his hair.

13

Mrs Duck went back to Old Ma Goat. What luck! Ma Goat had a smart cape and hood, just the right size for Derek.

Next time it rained, the Duck family shouted cheerfully, "Hurry up, Derek. Put on your cape and wellingtons."

"How's that, dear?" asked Mrs Duck.

"It's *lovely*, Mum," replied Derek.

Suddenly he saw a huge rainbow. "What's *that*?" he asked.

"That, my boy," said his father, "is a rainbow. A rainbow comes when the sun tries to shine through the rain."

"It's beautiful!" said Derek, gazing up at the bright colours. Then he looked around in wonder. Everything sparkled in the rain!

After that, Derek wanted it to rain every day. He didn't always see a rainbow. But he loved exploring in the rain. And sometimes he was in such a hurry to get started that he even forgot to put on his cape and wellingtons!

Mervyn's Glasses

It was dawn. Like all night birds, Mr and Mrs Owl were preparing for bed.

"I'm worried about Mervyn," said Mrs Owl. "I don't think he sees well."

"You worry too much, my dear," said Mr Owl, snuggling up to his wife. "Mervyn's just fine. Now you get a good day's sleep."

The Owl family slept all day. At dusk they woke up, and Mr Owl flew off to work.

All that night, Mrs Owl watched Mervyn carefully. She was right. Mervyn *couldn't* see well. He didn't always empty his plate. He held his new book too close to his eyes.

At bedtime Mrs Owl spoke to her husband again. "Tomorrow," she told him, "we must take Mervyn straight to Mr Specs. He'll soon put Mervyn right."

When Mervyn woke up, Mrs Owl explained the plan.

"But I don't want to wear glasses," said Mervyn. "They'll fall down my beak. They'll make me look silly."

"You'll look very handsome," Mrs Owl assured him. "Your father wears glasses, and there's nothing wrong with *his* looks!"

Mervyn enjoyed the visit to Mr Specs. Mr Specs tested his eyes with all kinds of charts and lenses. And Mervyn enjoyed choosing the frames for his glasses – it was fun seeing all the different shapes and colours they came in.

17

A week later, Mervyn and his mum went back to collect his glasses. Mr Specs held up a big mirror, and Mervyn saw himself clearly for the first time.

"What a fine bird I am!" he thought. "But I *don't* like my glasses!"

On the way home, Mervyn noticed all kinds of new things.

"Look at the stars!" he shouted. "And see those glow worms! These glasses work a treat."

But when he got home, Mervyn caught sight of himself in the mirror. "Silly old glasses!" he said to himself, stamping up and down his branch, crossly.

18

Just then the postman arrived. "Special delivery," he said, handing Mervyn a letter.

"What lovely big writing," said Mervyn. "It's an invitation," he told his parents, "to David's party. But I'm not going… *not in these glasses!*"

All week Mr and Mrs Owl tried to persuade Mervyn to change his mind. "Please go to the party," they said. "All your friends will be there. You don't want to disappoint David, do you?"

On the night of the party, Mervyn's dad tried one last time.

Mervyn shook his head.

"Well," said Dad, "if you don't want to play games and win prizes and eat a party tea, that's up to you. I only wish I could go!"

Mervyn started to think about all the other owls having fun. He thought about the sandwiches and lemonade and cake and ice cream. And in the end he decided to go to the party. He wrapped David's present and brushed his feathers. Then he flew there, all by himself.

David was waiting on his branch to greet Mervyn.

Mervyn landed gracefully and held out the present. And when he looked up at David, he got a super surprise.

David was wearing glasses, too. And he looked *so* handsome!

The Dirty Dinosaur

"Just look at your knees, Douglas!" cried Mrs Dinosaur.

"Brrm, brrm," said Douglas. He was much too busy with his car to look at his knees.

"Have you seen your face, Douglas?" asked Mr Dinosaur.

"Brrm, brrm," said Douglas. He was much too busy driving his car to look in the mirror.

"Don't you ever take a bath?" sighed Granny Dinosaur.

"Brrm, brrm," said Douglas. He *never* had time for a bath!

One day the Dinosaurs went to town. On their way, they passed
a sign. CAR WASH, it said, in big letters.

"Brrm, brrm!" said Douglas. And before you could say "diplodocus,"
he was inside.

"Douglas, come out of there!" cried Mum, Dad and Granny
Dinosaur.

But Douglas was having too much fun! "Ooooh!" he cried.
"It tickles… but I like it!"

At last Douglas came out of the car wash. "That was lovely!"
he said. And for the first time ever,
Douglas was clean… all over!

The Rainbow Rabbits

"Who's got my socks?" cried Mr Rabbit one morning. "Just wait until I find out which one of you naughty little bunnies has got them. Now then, Bayleaf – show me your feet!"

But the little rabbit just giggled. "I'm not Bayleaf, Dad," he said innocently. "I'm Bluebell. And these aren't *your* socks, they're Hazel's. And Hazel is wearing Scarlet's socks. And Scarlet is wearing Snowdrop's socks. And Rosebud isn't wearing any socks at all. And…"

"Stop!" cried Mr Rabbit. "You're making my ears spin!" He peered closely at the little bunny in front of him. "Are you *sure* you're not Bayleaf? No? Well, never mind. The point is that everything is in a muddle. No one knows who's wearing what, and I still haven't found my socks! There's only one answer to a mess like this – we need a *system*!"

Mrs Rabbit sighed. She remembered her husband's "Patent Improved Carrot-Cooking System" – the steam had peeled off all the wallpaper. And as for his "Water-Saving Ear-Washing System" – her ears had lost their wiggle for *weeks*!

Before long the floor was tail-deep in paper. "Don't stand on those charts!" cried Mr Rabbit, waving his crayons. "Now, everybody stand still and listen. My new system is based on *colour co-ordination*! And," he added modestly, "it's brilliant! What do you think?" he asked his wife.

"It's brilliant," said Mrs Rabbit, faintly.

In a few days Mr Rabbit's system was in operation. Little Scarlet was dressed from paws to ears all in red. Primrose was all in yellow. You can guess what happened to Bayleaf, Snowdrop, Hazel, Bluebell and Rosebud!

At first the seven little bunnies rather liked looking different from one another. But pretty soon they started to complain.

"I don't *like* brown," said Hazel. "I want a T-shirt like Bluebell's!"

"I'm never going to get dressed again if I have to wear horrible *green!*" wailed Bayleaf.

Mrs Rabbit could hardly think straight with all the complaining. But Mr Rabbit insisted that, with a few minor adjustments, everything would be fine.

He set to work again with his famous crayons. But at the end of the day, he accidentally left the crayons in his shirt pocket and then put the shirt in the washing machine with all the children's clothes.

24

When Mrs Rabbit took the washing out of the machine next morning, she laughed so loudly that the little rabbits came running. "What's the matter, Mum?" they asked.

Mrs Rabbit choked and sniffled. "I don't want to hear one more word about… ho ho ho… your clothes," she giggled. "Your father has… hee hee hee… invented a new system called… ha ha ha… the *Improved* Colour Co-ordination System – and we're *all* going to be using it!"

The little rabbits loved their multicoloured clothes.

"Well, it *was* time for… hh-hmm!… Phase Two of my System," said Mr Rabbit, looking aimlessly at the ceiling.

The Kitten
and the Kangaroo

The kitten and the kangaroo
Were bored and wondered what to do.
"I know," said Kanga, "take a ride!
Here's my pouch – just hop inside."

The kitten took a mighty leap.
"I say," she said, "you're mighty steep!"
"Come on," said Kanga, "grab a paw,
I'll take you on a guided tour."

The twosome bounced across the town.
"Gee-up!" said Kitten. "Don't slow down!"
But Kanga groaned, "I've had enough.
I'm high on bounce and low on puff."

"But I've no pouch," the kitten cried,
"To give my weary friend a ride."
She thought and sighed and thought some more,
Then rushed off to the superstore.

The boss was kind. He heard her plan.
"I'd like to help you if I can.
Here's a trolley – take good care –
I think your friend could fit in there."

So Kanga rode back home in style,
While Kitten pushed and gave a smile.
"I may be small, but you will find
I'll *never* leave a friend behind!"

An Up and Down Story

Mrs Kangaroo was on top of the world. She had a brand new baby. The baby was called Clifford.

Mrs Kangaroo rang up her friend. "Come and see my son," she said.

The friend hopped over right away. She brought a big book on child care. "I can give you some tips as well," she said. "With three children of my own, I know a thing or two."

Mrs Kangaroo listened to her friend's advice. She read the book carefully. More than anything, she wanted to be a good mother.

Clifford settled down quickly. He slept through the night. He gurgled through the day.

"Being a mum is easy," thought Mrs Kangaroo. "It's time to get out and about." She telephoned her friend. "We'll hop over for coffee," she said.

Mrs Kangaroo dressed Clifford in his best clothes and popped him into her pouch. Then she set off at top speed.

But before she got to the end of the road, Clifford started wailing. He'd never made such a dreadful noise before. Whatever could be the matter?

Mrs Kangaroo lifted Clifford out of her pouch and looked at him. She remembered everything she had read in her book, and she checked Clifford carefully. But he was clean and dry. He didn't have wind. She knew he couldn't be hungry, because she had just fed him.

Then Mrs Kangaroo noticed Clifford's face. It wasn't kangaroo-coloured at all. Clifford's face was a most awful shade of green!

Mrs Kangaroo was alarmed. Clifford must have the horrible disease the book had mentioned. It was called 'travel sickness', and it affected very young kangaroos who weren't used to their mother's hopping yet.

Sadly Mrs Kangaroo tiptoed the rest of the way to her friend's house. She went as smoothly as she could, but it's difficult for a kangaroo not to hop at all.

29

By the time Mrs Kangaroo arrived, Clifford was in bad shape. Mrs Kangaroo needed that cup of coffee.

"It's nothing to worry about," said her friend. "Just get some Bouncewell medicine for him."

Mrs Kangaroo went straight to the chemist's and bought some. "Put a teaspoonful in Clifford's next bottle," advised the chemist.

After Clifford's feed, Mrs Kangaroo set off hopefully for the shops. But the medicine didn't work. Clifford wailed all afternoon.

When she got home, Mrs Kangaroo rang her friend. "That medicine you told me about is no good," she complained. "Clifford's all green again, and I don't know *what* to do!"

"Don't worry," said her friend. "Lots of baby kangaroos get travel sickness. Clifford will soon grow out of it."

But Mrs Kangaroo couldn't wait for Clifford to grow out of it. She didn't want to be stuck at home all day. Being a mum wasn't so easy after all. Someone should have warned her.

That afternoon, while she was tidying the hall cupboard, Mrs Kangaroo found her old roller skates. As she looked at them, she began to get very excited. Could these be the answer to Clifford's problem?

The next day Mrs Kangaroo took Clifford for a trial run. She crossed her fingers for luck, because she didn't know *what* was going to happen.

Wheeee… Mrs Kangaroo set off down the street. She soon got the hang of her skates again. Clifford had never had such a smooth ride.

In no time at all Mrs Kangaroo was halfway across town. Clifford's face was still a beautiful kangaroo colour, and Mum wasn't stuck at home.

But Mrs Kangaroo was careful not to skate past the police station. She would hate to get arrested for speeding!

Slippy and the Skaters

There was once a bunny called Cowslip who was very clumsy. She bumped into furniture; she dropped her toast on the floor – jam side down – and she tripped over her own feet.

When Cowslip poured herself a drink, her mum would say, "Give that to me, Slippy. I'll carry it into the dining room. We don't want *more* milk in the pot plants, do we?"

Cowslip didn't mean to be careless. It was just that she didn't think about what she was doing. Her mind was always on something else.

At playgroup the little bunnies ran round the room to music.

> *Hoppity, skippety, JUMP!*
> *Hoppity, skippety, JUMP!*
> *Hoppity, skippety, BUMP!*

Yes, that was Cowslip. She'd noticed a spider high up on the ceiling and had forgotten to jump.

It seemed that hardly a day went by without Cowslip colliding with one of her friends or spilling her food – or without someone telling her to concentrate and *think* about what she was doing.

One winter the water in the village pond froze so hard that it was safe to skate on. All the little bunnies, and some of the big ones as well, whizzed and swooped across the ice. Cowslip went along too, and started to put on her skates.

"Oh Slippy, *please* don't come on the ice," shouted her brother. "You're sure to knock everyone over!"

"Perhaps you'd better just sit quietly on the bank and think, Slippy," advised her mum, who was practising her famous double-axel bunny-loop.

So Cowslip sat down on the bank and enjoyed watching her mum. She was a brilliant skater.

Soon the little bunny's mind moved on to other things. She noticed the way the ducks slithered and slipped on the ice, and wondered why they didn't wear skates. She noticed that old Bunny Hopkins was wearing odd socks and that his jacket didn't quite fit. She noticed that the ice was melting in the middle of the pond... *WHAT?*

"*STOP!*" cried Cowslip. "The ice is melting!"

In only a minute or two all the skaters were safely off the ice. Now they could see the growing hole in the middle, too.

"Well done, Slippy," said her mum. "You were the only one thinking about the really important things. If not for you, my double-axel bunny-loop – and your brothers and sisters – might never have been seen again!"

Chickens

We are the chickens,
(In case you hadn't guessed!)
We are the chickens,
We think you'll be impressed!

We slide down the haystack,
We balance on the coop,
We fly in strict formation
And *always* loop the loop!

We dive from the dovecote,
We stagger to a stop.
We like to chase the sheep,
And then to ride on top!

We bounce on the tractor,
We give the horn a *beep*!
We gallop round the yard,
And *never* go to sleep!

We are the chickens!
Our farmer needs a rest.
But still he tells his friends,
"MY CHICKENS ARE THE BEST!"

35

Brown Bear's Visit

Brown Bear had just finished breakfast. "That was horrible," he grumbled. "What's next?"

"Next," said Mum, "you can go to the playground while I tidy up."

At the playground, Brown Bear began to grizzle. "Same old friends, same old slide. It wouldn't be so bad if we had a climbing frame here!"

Brown Bear was grouchy all day. Then, when he got home, Mum sent him off to the waterfall for a shower.

"I hate getting clean!" he moaned. "Why can't I stay dirty sometimes?"

Brown Bear grumbled as he gobbled his supper. He grizzled as he snuggled into bed. Mum tucked him in and told him a story.

"That was boring," he yawned. Then he turned over and fell asleep.

Next morning Brown Bear had a visitor.
It was his cousin Billy Bear from
across the mountain.

"Can you come to play?" Billy
Bear asked. "Mum says you
can stay the night."

Brown Bear was so keen to go he
barely said goodbye to his mum. He didn't even wave to his
friends on the slide. He just jogged along beside his cousin and
asked what they were going to do first.

"First," said Billy Bear, "we'll go to the playground so I can show
you our climbing frame. Then I'll take you home to meet
the twins."

Brown Bear couldn't wait to try
the climbing frame. "It's easy,"
said Billy. "Just watch me and my
friends!" And they clambered up
to the top of the climbing frame
and began swinging from the
highest bars.

Brown Bear tried to do the same.
But he had never climbed so
high before. He fell off and
bumped his nose!

Billy didn't seem to notice.
He carried on climbing and
swinging with his friends until it
was time to go home.

As they neared home, Brown Bear smelt something cooking. The thought of food cheered him up. But Auntie was behind schedule.

"It's those twins," she explained. "They're always under my feet!"

But then she had a brainwave. "Why don't you big bears take the little ones to the river? You can bath them for me. And bath yourselves at the same time."

"I don't like rivers," said Brown Bear. "Why can't we go to the waterfall?"

"Because we don't have one," said Auntie simply, as she began to tidy up.

As soon as they reached the river, the twins squirted Brown Bear and Billy. Then, just when it was time to go home, they rolled on the bank and got all dirty again — and splashed mud all over Brown Bear and Billy. Brown Bear had *never* been so cross — or so hungry!

"Here you are at last," said Auntie, when they finally got home. But as soon as she brought in supper, the other bears swooped down like vultures. There was hardly anything at all left for Brown Bear.

Brown Bear's tummy was still rumbling when he went to bed. It was so dark he couldn't even see his cousins.

"Can I have a story?" he called out.

But Auntie was already snoring. And so were all the other bears.

The next day Billy led Brown Bear along the track. He pointed in the direction of Brown Bear's home. "Look," he said. "Your mum's coming to meet you."

Brown Bear barely said goodbye to his cousin. He bounded along the track as fast as his legs would carry him.

"It *is* good to see you, Brown Bear," said Mum. "Now, what would you like to do first?"

Brown Bear nestled up to Mum. He put his nose in the air and breathed in the sweet smells of home.

"Lovely friends! Lovely slide! Lovely waterfall! Lovely meals! Lovely stories!" he cried. "And I want to do it *all* first!"

The Puppy Who Went Exploring

Prudence the puppy was very excited. It had been such a thrilling day! She had started it living in one place, and now she was living somewhere completely different.

Her family had moved into a new house. Prudence couldn't wait to go exploring, even though she'd be going on her own. Her mum and dad and sister all said they had too much to do.

"See you later, everybody," she said, and trotted off.

"Don't get into any mischief, now," her dad called.

"Really," thought Prudence, "as if I would!"

Prudence went through the nearest door, and found herself approaching a cave full of interesting things. She snuffled inside it for a while, but then the things attacked her.

"Yikes!" said Prudence. "I'm off!"

She skidded into a nearby room, where she saw a strange box thing standing in the corner. She stood on her hind legs and sniffed at it... and suddenly it made a very loud noise!

"Yikes!" said Prudence. "I'm off!"

She scampered up the stairs and dashed into another room. There she found a big, puffy thing that was just right for biting and tugging... but it tried to smother her!

"Yikes!" said Prudence. "I'm off!"

She shot across the landing, rolled down the stairs, and landed at the bottom with a *bump*! And that's where the rest of the family found her when they came running.

"Prudence!" said her mum. "What *do* you think you're up to?"

"Quick, everybody," said Prudence breathlessly. "Let's get out of here before it's too late…"

When they'd stopped laughing, Prudence's family showed her round the house. She discovered that the cave was a broom cupboard, the box thing was a television, and the puffy thing a duvet. To make her feel more cheerful, Prudence's dad found her a bone. And next time she went exploring — she didn't go alone!

The Trouble With Babies

One day Timmy's mum sat him on her knee. "Timmy," she said, "soon you are going to have some little brothers and sisters to play with. Won't that be nice?"

Timmy was very excited. He was tired of playing all by himself and he could hardly wait for the new bunnies to be born. He tidied up his toy box and started to think of good games he could play with his brothers and sisters.

He lined up all his cars and his big yellow tractor under the table. "This can be Timmy's Garage," he thought. "The little bunnies can drive my cars, and I will be Chief Mechanic."

"Come and see your new brothers and sisters!" said Timmy's dad a few days later. Mum was sitting up in bed holding four little bundles. Timmy tiptoed forward.

"But they're tiny!" he squeaked in surprise. They certainly didn't look big enough to drive his big yellow tractor.

"They'll grow very fast," laughed Mum.

But the babies didn't grow very fast at all. They were still tiny the next day, and the day after that. They seemed to be asleep nearly all the time – and they wouldn't even open their eyes!

A few weeks later the little bunnies started to smile and gurgle. Timmy waited until his mum was out of the room.

"It's all right," he whispered to his brothers and sisters. "She's not here. You can stop pretending now and talk to me." But the little bunnies just smiled and gurgled some more.

"Come and see my garage," said Timmy. But the little bunnies didn't seem at all interested.

Mum found Timmy looking sad. "My new brothers and sisters don't like me," he said. "They won't talk to me, and they don't want to share my toys."

"But Timmy," said his mum, "that's because they're only a few weeks old, and you are a big bunny now. They have a lot to learn, and *you* can help me teach them to do all the things that you can do."

So Timmy put away his cars and his big yellow tractor. "Little bunnies are not ready to play with big toys yet," he announced. "They have a lot to learn."

Then he piled some cushions and his picture books under the table. "This is Timmy's School," he said. "And I am the Baby Bunny Teacher!"

Mrs Bunny Had Twins

What wonderful news!
But what names would she choose?
So many relatives
Had their own views.

Said old Uncle Boris,
"Have you thought of Horace?
And Doris? Or Morris?
Or Norris? Or... *Boris?*"

Smiled Grandmother Connie,
"Dear, what about Ronnie?
And Bonnie? Or Jonnie?
Or Lonnie? Or... *Connie?*"

Cried young Cousin Harry,
"But what about Barry?
And Carrie? Or Larry?
Or Gary? Or... *Harry?*"

Laughed poor Mrs Bunny,
"Here's Sonny. Here's Honey.
For names don't sound funny,
When they rhyme with... *Bunny!*"

The Roly Poly Kitten

Once upon a time there was a Roly Poly Kitten. He was friendly, he was cheerful and, although he didn't know it, he was just a little plump.

One day it rained so hard that the Roly Poly Kitten had to stay indoors. All morning he chased his brothers and sisters.

At last lunchtime came. "Now, sit down," said Dad, "and please eat nicely."

The Roly Poly Kitten bounced up to his place and tucked in. But the other kittens grumbled at him.

"Move over," cried one. "You're taking up all the room!"

"Hey!" squealed another. "You're sitting on my tail!"

But the smallest kitten yelled loudest of all. "Go away!" she cried. "You're a FAT KITTEN, and I can't reach the food!"

Whooooosh! The Roly Poly Kitten ran right out of the house and down the lane, where he hid under a hedge. "I'm fat! I'm fat!" he sniffed. "And nobody likes me." Then he took a deep breath and tried to look thinner – but that only gave him hiccups.

Back home, Dad was worried. "We shall have to make a search party," he announced.

"Oooh, I LOVE parties!" squealed the smallest kitten.

But Dad looked stern. "What I mean," he explained, "is that we must find your brother."

So the kittens went outside to search, and eventually they reached the hedge where the Roly Poly Kitten was hiding. A stranger happened to be walking by.

"I'm looking for my son," Dad told her. "Perhaps you've seen him. Let me describe him for you."

"Oh no!" thought the Roly Poly Kitten. He didn't want to hear how fat he was. But his family shouted so loudly that he *had* to listen.

"He's friendly!"

"He's cheerful!"

"He's handsome!"

"He's strong!"

"He's…" the smallest kitten thought carefully, "he's CUDDLY!"

"That's right," smiled Dad. "He's a very special kitten indeed."

The Roly Poly Kitten was too surprised to speak.

The stranger said she was very sorry, but she hadn't seen him. "Goodness me," sighed Dad. "Wherever can he be?" In the end he and the other kittens went to look at home.

Inside the house, all was still and quiet. But not for long.

Whoooosh! The Roly Poly Kitten sprang out of his hiding place "I feel friendly!" he announced, bounding through the door. "I feel cheerful! I feel handsome! I feel strong! I feel cuddly! But most of all," he cried as he sat down at the table, "I feel… HUNGRY!"

Teamwork

Two leopards were wearing
    A terrible frown.
They wriggled and jiggled
    And jumped up and down.

They twisted, insisted,
    "I *can* count my spots."
Then tumbled and grumbled,
    "I'm tied up in knots!"

They growled and they scowled,
    They hadn't a clue.
Then, all of a sudden,
    They knew what to do.

They bounced and announced,
    As they shook their great paws,
"You can count *my* spots…
    And I will count *yours*!"

51

Flop Learns to Swim

Flop, the penguin, was nervous. It was time for his first swimming lesson.

"Hurry up!" called Dad at the top of his voice. "We don't want to be late."

"Hey! What about breakfast?" cried Flop. He was hoping he could distract Dad, and then maybe he would forget about swimming.

But Dad just said, "No breakfast till after swimming. Swimming on a full stomach will give you cramp."

Down by the sea Flop got cold feet. He tugged at Dad's flipper. "The water's *f-f-f-freezing!*" he said. "Let's go home for breakfast."

Dad took no notice. "The first thing to learn about swimming," he began, "is to relax."

But Flop didn't feel relaxed. He felt cold and wobbly. "What if I can't do it, Dad?" he whispered. "Everyone will laugh."

Just then a group of young penguins rushed past him. "Watch this, Flop!" they cried.

One by one, the penguins dived into the sea — *splish, splash, splosh* — covering Flop with spray.

"Brrrrrr! Brrrrrr!" Flop's beak began to chatter. "Please, Dad," he said, "I want to go home."

But Dad was beginning to enjoy himself. "Never mind them," he said. "Watch *me!*"

Flop shivered miserably on the shore and watched as Dad began his demonstration.

"Deep, *splish*, breaths, *splosh*," Dad gasped. "Chin, *splish*, up, *splosh*," he called. "Now *you* try, Flop!"

Flop took a deep breath and waded towards Dad. But he tripped and fell beak-first into the water.

"HELP! HELP!" yelled Flop. "I'M DROWNING!"

Dad scooped Flop out of the water. He patted him firmly on the back.

Flop choked and spluttered. "I don't want to do any more swimming today," he whispered.

Now it was Dad's turn to choke and splutter. "Call *that* swimming?" he bellowed. "For heaven's sake, Flop, please try and concentrate!"

54

Flop tried harder and harder to swim. Dad tried harder and harder to teach him. But the harder Dad tried, the louder he shouted.

"Please, Dad," said Flop. "I'm not *deaf*. I just can't swim."

Dad gave a huge sigh and one last demonstration. But it was no use. Flop just couldn't do it.

Dad waddled back to the shore. He sat down with a plop – the picture of disappointment.

Just at that moment, another father arrived in the bay. His young daughter was swimming strongly beside him.

Flop's dad groaned and put his head in his flippers.

Flop felt so sorry for his father that he did a very brave thing. He bobbed carefully out to sea until the water reached right up to his beak. Then he swam along… with one foot on the bottom.

"Look at me! Look at me!" quavered Flop.

"WELL DONE, FLOP!" cried Dad, beaming. He started to strut proudly along the shore.

"Well done!" said the other dad. Then he took a closer look at Flop's father.

"Why, it's old Shortie!" he boomed. "I haven't seen you since those *terrible* swimming lessons. Don't you remember? Our fathers nearly deafened us. In the end we went along with one foot on the bottom – just to keep them happy!"

"*Ahem! Ahem! Ahem!*" For some strange reason Flop's dad couldn't stop coughing.

Flop was fascinated. Fancy that penguin calling his dad "Shortie". And fancy Dad swimming along with *his* foot on the bottom!

Flop began to feel more relaxed. He wriggled his toes in the water and gave a little chortle. Then, all of a sudden, he gave a great *whoop* of delight.

"I'M SWIMMING! I'M SWIMMING!" he cried. And, as he shouted, Flop flipped onto his back and waved both feet in the air… just to prove it!

Dance of the Dolphins

Slow, slow, quick quick, slow,
Ride the waves,
And here we go.

Quick, quick, leap up high,
Arch your back,
It's time to fly!

Fly, fly, puff and blow,
Blow some bubbles
In a row.

Puff, puff, waltz and spin,
Shake your tail,
Flick your fin.

Slow, slow, quick quick, slow,
Take a partner,
Dive down low.

Quick, quick, slow slow, quick,
Listen carefully,
That's the trick!

Cry Bunny
and Scaredy Cat

There was once a timid little rabbit named Daisy, and she cried a lot. *Boo-hoo*, all day long, because she was so frightened and so terribly shy.

"If only I had a friend," she used to say, "things would be different."

But no one wanted to be Daisy's friend, because she cried so much. They teased her instead, and called her a Cry Bunny.

"Cry Bunny, Shy Bunny,
Go away!
Cry Bunny, Shy Bunny,
You can't play!"

They all laughed together as Daisy wandered off alone, looking for something to do by herself.

One day Daisy stood behind a tree watching the others have fun. She saw them skipping and climbing and bouncing balls. They were laughing and calling out to one another as they ran and played. They were having a good time, but Daisy was feeling unhappy, as usual.

Then Daisy heard something that sounded familiar. Teasing voices were shouting,

> "Scaredy Cat, Scaredy Cat,
>   Go away!
> Scaredy Cat, Scaredy Cat,
>   You can't play!"

Everyone was pointing at Roger Cat. He was walking away with his head down, brushing tears from his eyes.

"How can they be so mean?" thought Daisy. She forgot all about being shy, and hurried over to Roger and smiled at him.

"I'll be your friend," she said. "I'll play with you."

Roger looked up. "Oh thank you, Daisy!" he said. "I'll be your friend, too."

So off they went, Daisy and Roger, far from the others.

Next morning Daisy and Roger walked to the stream. First they had a game of tag on the grassy bank. Then they went fishing and caught a little silver trout.

Next day Roger and Daisy played together again, and the day after that. They found all sorts of good things to do together. One day they played school. Another day they pretended to be pirates on the high seas. They became best friends, and never even thought about crying or being scared.

One afternoon while they were playing in the wood, heavy rain clouds filled the sky. Suddenly Daisy and Roger were caught in a downpour.

As they were hurrying home, they heard a small voice crying, "Help! Help!"

It was hard to see in the heavy rain, but Daisy finally spotted Stanley Squirrel's baby brother stuck in the branch of a tree.

"Don't be afraid!" called Daisy. "We'll get you out!"

The tree was too wet and slippery to climb, so Daisy stood on Roger's shoulders. She reached up and pulled the little squirrel out of the branch. Then, holding him carefully, she slid to the ground and carried him home.

"Oh Daisy," said Mrs Squirrel when she heard what had happened, "how brave of you and Roger!"

She gave her little son a hug, dried him off, and then made Daisy and Roger a cup of cocoa.

Before long everyone had heard about Daisy and Roger's daring rescue.

"I suppose Daisy isn't a Cry Bunny any more," said Rosie Fox.

"And Roger isn't a Scaredy Cat after all," said Stanley Squirrel.

"I hope they can play with us tomorrow," said Bonnie Badger.

So Daisy and Roger, who used to get teased for being frightened and shy, turned out to be quite brave and bold after all. And soon they had lots of friends.

Best of all, nobody ever called them Cry Bunny or Scaredy Cat again.

The Dancing Bunny

Do you know young Hoppy
Who never can keep still?
If you haven't seen him,
Then you certainly will.

He jigs in the sunshine,
He hops in the drizzle,
He zooms out of the house
With a double-toed twizzle.

From breakfast to supper
He dances and jiggles,
He waggles and waltzes,
He prances and wiggles.

And when sleepy Hoppy
Is tucked up in bed,
He's dancing the fox-trot
Inside his own head!

The Runaway Mouse

"I'm just popping out for some supper," said Mrs Mouse.

A few minutes later, she staggered back with a huge hunk of cheese.

"Ooooh!" squeaked five small voices. "Please can we have some now, Mum?"

"No," said Mrs Mouse. "This cheese is for supper."

But the smallest mouse couldn't wait. When no one was looking, she took a big, big bite.

Mmmmmm! The cheese tasted wonderful! So she took another bite, and another… until Mum caught her.

"Bed!" cried Mrs Mouse. "And no more cheese for a week!"

The little mouse felt so sorry for herself that she bolted right out of their hole and into the big wide farmyard.

64

"Watch out!" cried a cross voice. It belonged to a puppy.

"I'm running away," the little mouse told him. "Mum shouted at me. She said I couldn't have any more cheese."

"But did she stop you playing football?" asked the puppy.

The little mouse looked surprised and shook her head.

"Well, think yourself lucky," said the puppy. "Mine did, just because I was a bit rough with my little brother. Would *you* like to be goalkeeper?"

The little mouse took one look at the tangle of puppies on the grass and carried on running. She ran so fast that she almost fell into the duck pond.

"Going for a swim?" quacked a glum voice. The little mouse shook her head.

"Nor me," said the duckling. "I'm not allowed in today, just because I was a bit cheeky. But I could teach *you* how to dive."

The little mouse looked at the other ducklings swimming in the deep, cold pond, and she shivered. Then she carried on running.

"Not so fast!" hissed a black and white calf.

"I can't stop!" squeaked the little mouse. "I'm running away. Because Mum shouted."

"I wish I could shout!" hissed the calf. "I mooed a bit too loudly last night, and now I'm only allowed to *whisper*!"

"Wow! Was all that noise *you*?" cried the little mouse. "You woke everyone up. We were so frightened that Mum had to bring us a midnight feast and tell us another…"

Suddenly the little mouse felt so homesick that she ran — *whoosh* — all the way back to her hole. She dived straight into bed with her brothers and sisters, and was just in time for a… story!

The Chewalong Song

Chew, chew, I *do* love a chew!
There's nothing like breakfast
All covered in dew.
There's no need to buy it,
Or even to fry it,
So why don't you try it
And *chew*!

Munch, munch, I *do* love a munch!
There's nothing like clover
For flavouring lunch.
Although it grows thickly
You won't find it sickly,
So gather some quickly
And *munch*!

Graze, graze, I *do* love a graze!
There's nothing quite like it
On warm, sunny days.
So please share my dinner,
This field is a winner!
We'll never grow thinner,
Let's *graze*!

A Balloon for Katie Kitten

Katie Kitten loved balloons. When she saw the balloon man in the park, she squealed with delight.

"Please, Mum," she begged, "*please* buy me a balloon."

But Mum wasn't sure. "Those balloons are filled with a gas called helium," she told Katie. "You have to hold on to them very tightly. If you let go, they just float away. Do you think you're grown up enough for a helium balloon?"

"Yes," said Katie, "I *am* grown up enough. *Please* may I have one? I'd like *that* one!" She pointed to a panda balloon.

Mum sighed and got out her purse. The balloon man beamed and unwound Panda's string. He wanted to tie the string round Katie's wrist, but Katie couldn't wait. She ran round and round the park with Panda, whooping and shouting joyfully.

"Hold tight, Katie Kitten!" warned Mum.

But… *whoosh!* Mum's warning was too late. Panda was already floating up into a tree.

Katie didn't like heights, but she bravely climbed the tree and rescued Panda. Mum waited anxiously below.

"I thought you might not be grown up enough," said Mum, when Katie was safely on the ground again. "Now, let me hold Panda. We have shopping to do."

69

When they got to the department store, Katie grabbed Panda's string and jumped on the escalator. As they rode upstairs, they had a wonderful view of all the things for sale on each floor.

"Wow, look at those toys!" cried Katie. She pointed to a row of dinosaurs, and... *whoosh!* Off went Panda again.

Panda flew past the toys. He flew past the lamps. He flew past the pots and pans, and came to rest right at the top of the store.

At last Mum and Katie got to the top, too.

"I thought you might not be grown up enough..." began Mum.

"There's Panda!" cried Katie. "He's sitting on one of the hats!"

The shop assistant looked very stern. But Katie bravely walked up to her and asked, very politely, if she could get her balloon.

They were just in time. A woman was pointing to the display and asking if she could try on "the cute hat with the panda on top"!

Katie held Panda very tightly while Mum did her shopping. She hung on hard while they waited for the bus. And when they walked up Katie's street, she decided to wrap the string round her wrist.

"Panda can live in my room," she told Mum.

Suddenly baby Jack from next door ran over to greet them. Jack laughed and pointed at Panda. But then he tripped and bumped his nose!

Katie ran to pick him up. "Don't cry, Jack," she said, and gave him a hug.

WHOOSH!

"Oh no!" cried Katie. Panda was floating far, far away. And this time there was nothing to stop him!

As soon as Jack stopped crying, Katie ran inside and shut herself in her room. She wouldn't come downstairs for supper. She didn't want to read or draw or play dominoes.

Brr-ring! went the doorbell. When Katie heard it, she hid her head under her pillow.

After a while, Mum called upstairs, "Katie, there's a visitor here to see you."

But Katie just sniffled and replied, "I'm not… grown up enough… for visitors!"

"Nonsense!" boomed a friendly voice. It was Grandpa Purr. Mum had told him all about their adventures.

"If you're grown up enough to climb a tree without getting hurt," said Grandpa, "and to speak politely to a stern shop assistant, and to comfort baby Jack – then you're grown up enough for me!"

Katie thought about what Grandpa had said. She began to feel a bit better. At last she came downstairs.

"Hold tight, Katie Kitten," said Grandpa. He opened his arms wide to scoop her up and give her a cuddle. But he let go of the balloon he had brought her!

Whooosh! Elephant floated all the way upstairs, right into Katie's room. Grandpa, Mum and Katie all looked at one another and started laughing.

"Oh, Grandpa," cried Katie, "I don't think you're grown up enough for a helium balloon!"

Just the Job for a Dragon

Dilys read the advertisement in the café window:

WANTED
Smart
young lady
to wait
at table

"Just the job for a dragon," thought Dilys, and she stepped inside.

The café manager wasn't so sure. "We'll have to see how you get on," he said.

Dilys helped the cook to peel the potatoes. Then she flew round setting the tables.

At twelve o'clock the first customers arrived. "Oh no," said the manager. "It's the Grumble family! They're never satisfied with *anything!*"

Dilys wasn't worried. She stood by their table with a notepad and pencil, ready to take their orders.

"I can feel a draught," said Grandma Grumble. "It's right on my feet."

"I *am* sorry, Madam," said Dilys. She lifted the cloth and took a deep breath… PUFF!… Dilys blew hot air all over Grandma Grumble's toes.

"Ooh, that's lovely!" gurgled Grandma Grumble.

The Grumbles read the menu. "It all sounds horrible," said Mr Grumble. But they ordered a huge meal, just the same.

Dilys brought out their plates. Mr and Mrs Grumble poked and prodded. "These plates are cold!" they cried. "Hot food should be served on hot plates!"

"I do apologise, sir *and* madam," said Dilys. She collected all the plates and turned her back. *Puff!* She aimed a great flame right at the plates, and took them back to the table.

"Ouch!" cried Mr and Mrs Grumble. "That's better! These plates are piping hot now!"

When the Grumbles had finished their main course, Sidney wanted his pudding.

"Bring me a Spaceship Special," he cried. "Banana, jelly, ice cream, syrup, nuts…"

The cook made up the Spaceship Special – but he forgot to light the sparkler on top.

"My sparkler's not lit!" wailed Sidney.

"Oh yes, it is!" said Dilys. *Puff!* She sent a gentle flame right onto the spaceship, and the sparkler crackled into life.

"Crikey!" said Sidney.

The Grumbles paid their bill with hardly a grumble, and Dilys began to clear the table.

"What do you think?" she asked the manager when she had finished.

"I think," said the manager, "that this is *just the job for a dragon!*"

Everard's Ears

Once there was a bunny called Everard who had extra-large ears.

"Everard, your ears are *enormous!*" laughed his friends Basil and Beech.

Everard's ears started drooping, and he looked very unhappy.

"It's all right, son," said Everard's dad. "You just haven't grown into your ears yet. And who knows – one day you may find they come in useful."

But Everard couldn't think of a single thing that big ears would ever be useful for. And it seemed his friends would *never* stop teasing him.

"Shouldn't you put flashing lights on your ears to warn low-flying aircraft?" asked Basil.

"No wonder there's a hole in the ozone layer!" giggled Beech.

Everard's ears drooped down even further.

"Ears up, son," said Everard's dad. "Any rabbit can have ordinary ears, but you're my *extraordinary* Everard. And don't you forget it!"

Now, there was a big cabbage field nearby, and whenever there was washing up or bedroom tidying to be done, Everard, Basil and Beech would hop off into the field to hide. They would sit among the huge cabbages, nibbling leaves or playing games, and wait until they thought it was safe to go home.

One afternoon in the cabbage field, Beech started laughing. "Everard!" he giggled, holding two big cabbage leaves above his head. "What do these remind you of?"

Everard didn't think it was funny. He chased Beech through the cabbages until they were both out of breath.

"Stop!" puffed Basil, trailing along behind. "Where are we?" The cabbages had grown so high that the bunnies couldn't see which way to go.

After what seemed like hours of running in all directions, the three bunnies were near to tears. "We'll be here for *ever*!" said Beech. "I'm sorry, Everard, it's all my fault!"

The frightened little bunnies were exhausted and flopped down among the cabbages. "No one will ever find us," sobbed Basil. "But if we ever do get out, we promise never to make fun of you-know-what again, Everard!"

A few minutes later they heard a cheery voice nearby. "Come on, boys," said Everard's dad. "I'll show you the way home. It's lucky I reached you before it got dark."

"How ever did you find us?" asked Beech, as they all tramped home together.

Everard's dad looked down at his son's ears waving above the cabbages. He gave Everard a big wink. "Let's just say I had *extraordinary* good luck," he said.

Scaredy Kitten

On the night before Christmas, Prescott was all bundled up, ready to go carol singing with his sister Sylvia and their friends. He opened the front door and peered outside.

"Gosh!" he thought. "It's dark. Very dark."

"It's too cold for me," Prescott said to Sylvia.

"It is not," Sylvia said. "You're just afraid of the dark. What a scaredy kitten!"

82

Prescott went to his room and took off his scarf and hat and mittens and boots. He put on his pyjamas, turned on his night light and crawled into bed.

"Oh no!" he said suddenly. "How could I forget?"

He got out of bed and pulled the window blind down tight. Then he drew the curtains, to make sure he couldn't see the night.

Prescott *was* afraid of the dark. He couldn't tell where the darkness ended and everything else began. He felt as if he were disappearing in the dark. And that made him very nervous.

Most of the time it didn't matter that Prescott was afraid of the dark. But sometimes it mattered a lot.

On Halloween, Prescott got into his ghost costume, ready for trick-or-treating. He thought that maybe the bright white sheet would help keep him from disappearing in the dark.

But when he stepped outside, he saw that it was rainy and foggy, and *very* dark. *Everything* had disappeared!

"It's too wet for me," said Prescott, going back inside.

"Scaredy kitten!" said Sylvia.

Prescott stayed indoors that night and greeted the other trick-or-treaters at the door. They were all smiling or laughing. Prescott hid his sad face behind his mask.

Just a few days later it was Bonfire Night. Everyone was going to the village green to watch the fireworks. Everyone except Prescott.

"I'm too sleepy," said Prescott, pretending to yawn. "Maybe I'll watch from my bedroom window."

"Scaredy kitten!" said Sylvia.

Prescott went up to his room and tried to watch the fireworks from the window. But he ended up turning on his night light, pulling the blind down and drawing the curtains to keep out the night. He never saw any fireworks at all.

A few weeks later it was Prescott's birthday. His grandpa came to his party and brought a special present. When Prescott opened the box, he didn't know what it was.

"This is a telescope," Grandpa explained. "You take it outside at night and look through it to see the sky up close. You'll be surprised when you see what's up there. But we have to wait until it's dark."

Prescott didn't want to be surprised in the dark. He didn't want to go outside at night at all.

"Scaredy kitten," whispered Sylvia. "I bet you don't go!"

But Prescott loved Grandpa very much, and he couldn't disappoint him. So when it got dark, he went outside with Grandpa and the telescope. He held Grandpa's hand very tightly.

Grandpa showed Prescott how to hold the telescope up to his eye and look up at the sky. "Just look through it and tell me what you see," he said to Prescott.

86

Prescott looked.

"I see stars," he said. "Oh! Look at them! They're so shiny! And look at the moon! The moon is so bright! It's like a huge torch! Wow!"

Prescott was amazed. And when he took the telescope away from his eye, the night didn't seem so dark any more.

"Is the moon there every night?" he asked.

"Yes," replied Grandpa. "On cloudy or foggy nights you can't see the moon or the stars, but they're always there. You can count on them!"

"I can?" Prescott asked.

Grandpa smiled. "Yes," he said. "I knew you'd be surprised. I'll bet you didn't know there was so much light in the night."

When Prescott went to bed that night, he didn't turn on his night light or pull down his window blind or draw the curtains. The stars shone in the window and the moon gleamed brightly.

Prescott smiled as he watched the light of the night glowing in his room. He wasn't afraid of the dark any more.

The Puppy
Who Wanted to Be a Cat

Life seemed far too busy for Penny the puppy. There was always something her parents wanted her to do, and she was fed up with it. So one day, Penny decided to be... a cat.

"Cats can do whatever they like," Penny said to her brother and sister. "I mean, just look at Ginger!"

Penny and her family shared the house with Ginger the cat. He did an awful lot of dozing and was never, ever, in a hurry.

"But you're a dog," said Penny's brother. "You can't be a cat."

"Oh, can't I?" said Penny. "We'll soon see about that!"

From then on, Penny copied everything Ginger did. She walked like a cat, stretched out on the rug like a cat, and even tried to miaow like a cat, although that was quite hard.

And when her parents told her to do something, she said, "I'm sorry, I can't do that. I'm a cat!"

As you can imagine, after a while this started to drive her parents *crazy*. So they came up with a plan...

The next morning there was a surprise for Penny. At breakfast, her brother's bowl was full of lovely, chunky dog food, and so was her sister's. But Penny's contained something rather strange.

"What's *this?*" asked Penny, sniffing at it.

"Well, since you're a cat now," said her mother, "we thought you ought to have cat food for your meals!"

Suddenly Penny wasn't so sure being a cat was such a good idea. How could Ginger eat this disgusting stuff? It was so *yucky*…

The rest of the family burst out laughing at the look on Penny's face. Penny laughed too when her father took away the bowl of cat food and produced a proper breakfast for her.

And from then on Penny was a puppy again. At least she was — until she saw a bird flying through the sky.

"Don't be absurd," said her sister. "You can't be a bird!"

But Penny's parents wouldn't put anything past her.

And neither would I!

Crocodiles *Do* Climb Trees

"**D**on't do that, Mum," said Snappy. "Crocodiles aren't meant to dance. They're meant to slither and be menacing."

But Snappy's mum didn't want to slither. And she didn't feel at all menacing.

"Slow, slow, quick quick, slow," she hummed as she danced up to a bush filled with flowers. She picked a bright red flower and put it behind her ear.

Snappy groaned. "Leave it out, Mum. What if any of my friends see you?"

Snappy's mum didn't mind *who* saw her. She carried on dancing all afternoon. Then, instead of slithering in a nice, menacing sort of way, she shot up the nearest tree.

"Mum, Mum!" shrieked Snappy. "Crocodiles *don't* climb trees!"

"This one does," said Mum. "It makes me feel good. And I like the view."

Snappy stomped off to the river bank and sulked.

"Come on in!" called a voice from the water. "It's a lovely day for a dip."

Snappy slithered down the bank. He liked the look of this new friend.

"He's just my sort of croc," thought Snappy. And, before he knew it, Snappy had invited him over… the next afternoon.

All night long Snappy worried and wriggled. However could he make his mum behave in front of his new friend? At last he thought of a plan.

At the crack of dawn, Snappy swung into action.

"Wake up, Mum!" he cried. "We'll dance all morning!" That way, Snappy thought, she would be too tired to dance that afternoon!

"Slow, slow, quick quick, slow." Snappy and his mum danced themselves dizzy until lunchtime.

"Let's have lunch in that tree!" cried Snappy. That way, he thought, she wouldn't need to climb it later.

Snappy got Mum back on the ground just in time. "I think I hear someone coming!" he said. "Now please, Mum, remember: crocodiles *don't* climb trees!"

"This one does!" boomed a friendly voice.

Snappy couldn't believe his ears. It was his new friend's mum!

"Slow, slow, quick quick, slow!" She was dancing along in front of her son to show him the way.

Snappy's new friend groaned and blushed. But Snappy gave his widest grin.

"We're going swimming!" he called over his shoulder, as he and his friend slithered off to the river.

But, of course, Snappy's mum didn't hear him. She was too busy showing *her* new friend the view… from her favourite treetop!